DATE DUE

Lieutenant Gustl

WITHDRAWN

MASTERWORKS OF FICTION

Our advisory board

Tereza Albues [Brazil]
Jorge Amado [Brazil]
Mulk Raj Anand [India]
Paul Auster [USA]
G. Cabrera Infante [Cuba]
Marcel Cohen [France]
Guy Davenport [USA]
Lydia Davis [USA]
Mohammed Dib [Algeria]
Per Olav Enquist [Sweden]
Raymond Federman
    [France/USA]
Liliane Giraudon [France]
Jaimy Gordon [USA]
Juan Goytisolo [Spain]
Charles Juliet [France]
Steve Katz [USA]

Roger Laporte [France]
Doris Lessing [England]
Nathaniel Mackey [USA]
Luigi Malerba [Italy]
Friederike Mayröcker
    [Austria]
Harry Mathews [USA/France]
Harry Mulisch
    [The Netherlands]
Péter Nádas [Hungary]
José Emilio Pacheco [Mexico]
Susan Sontag [USA]
Gilbert Sorrentino [USA]
Thorvald Steen [Norway]
Robert Steiner [USA]
Michel Tournier [France]
Wendy Walker [USA]

Douglas Messerli, Publisher

Arthur Schnitzler

Lieutenant Gustl

Translated from the German by Richard L. Simon

MASTERWORKS OF FICTION
(1901)

BENEDICTINE UNIVERSITY LIBRARY
IN THE KINDLON HALL OF LEARNING
5700 COLLEGE ROAD
LISLE, IL 60532-0900
1

GREEN INTEGER
KØBENHAVEN & LOS ANGELES
2003

GREEN INTEGER
Edited by Per Bregne
København / Los Angeles

Distributed in the United States by Consortium Book
Sales and Distribution, 1045 Westgate Drive, Suite 90
Saint Paul, Minnesota 55114-1065

(323) 857-1115 / http://www.greeninteger.com

First published by Green Integer in 2003
Originally published in 1901
Biographical information ©2003 by Green Integer

Design: Per Bregne
Typography & Cover: Trudy Fisher
Photograph: Arthur Schnitzler

LIBRARY OF CONGRESS CATALOGING IN PUBLICATION DATA
Schnitzler, Arthur [1862-1931]
Lieutenant Gustl
ISBN: 1-931243-46-8
p. cm — Green Integer 85
I. Title II. Series III. Translator

Green Integer Books are published for Douglas Messerli
Printed in the United States of America on acid-free paper.

Without limiting the rights under copyright reserved here, no part
of this publication may be reproduced, stored in or introduced into
a retrieval system, or transmitted, in any form or by any means
(electronic, mechanical, photocopying, recording or otherwise),
without the prior written permission of both the copyright owner
and the above publisher of the book.

How long is this thing going to last? Let's see what time it is . . . perhaps I shouldn't look at my watch at a serious concert like this. But no one will see me. If anyone does, I'll know he's paying just as little attention as I am. In that case I certainly won't be embarrassed . . . . Only quarter to ten? . . . I feel as though I'd been here for hours. I'm just not used to going to concerts . . . . What's that they're playing? I'll have a look at the program . . . . Yes that's what it is: an oratorio. Thought it was a mass. That sort of thing belongs in church, and in church only. There's one advantage that church has over a concert: you can leave whenever you want to. — I wish I were sitting on the aisle! Steady, steady! Even oratorios end some time. Perhaps this one's very beautiful, and I'm just in the wrong mood. Well, why not? When I think that I came here for diversion . . . I should have given my ticket to Benedek. He likes this sort of thing. Plays violin. But in that case Kopetzsky would have felt insulted. It was very nice of him; meant well, at least. He's a good fellow,

Kopetzsky! The only one I can really trust . . . . His sister is singing up there on the platform. There are at least a hundred women up there — all of them dressed in black. How am I to know which one is Kopetzsky's sister? They gave him a ticket because she was singing in the chorus . . . . Why then, didn't Kopetzsky go? —They're singing rather nicely now. It's inspiring! Bravo! Bravo! . . . Yes, I'll applaud along with the rest of them. The fellow next to me is clapping as if he were crazy. Wonder if he really likes it as much as all that? — Pretty girl over there in the box! Is she looking at me or at the man with the blond beard? . . . Ah, here we have a solo! Who is it? ALTO: FRÄULEIN WALKER, SOPRANO: FRÄULEIN MICHALEK . . . that one is probably the soprano . . . I haven't been at the opera for an awfully long time. Opera always amuses me, even when it's dull. I might go again the day after tomorrow. They're playing Traviata. No, day after tomorrow I'll probably be dead! Oh, nonsense; I can't even believe that myself! Just wait, Doctor, you'll stop making remarks like that! You'll get what's coming to you! . . .

I wish I could see the girl in the box more clearly. I'd like to borrow an opera glass. But this fellow next to me would probably eat me if I broke in on his reveries . . . . Wonder where Kopetzsky's sister is sitting? Wonder if I'd recognize her? I've met her only two or three times, the last time at the Officers' Club. Wonder if they're all good girls, all hundred of them? Oh, Lord! . . . ASSISTED BY THE SINGING CLUB — Singing Club . . . that's a good one! I'd always imagined that members of a Singing Club would be something like Vienna chorus girls; that is, I might have known they'd be nothing like them at all! Pleasant recollection! That time at Green Gate . . . What was her name? And then she once sent me a post card from Belgrade . . . that's a good place too! Well, Kopetzsky's lucky right now, sitting in the café, smoking a good cigar!

Why's that fellow staring at me all the time? I suppose he notices how bored I am . . . I'll have you know that if you keep on looking fresh like that I'll meet you in the lobby later and settle with you! He's looking the other way already! They're all afraid of my eyes . . . "You have the most beautiful eyes I've ever seen!" Steffi said that the other day . . . . Oh Steffi, Steffi, Steffi! — It's Steffi's fault that I'm sitting here bored by the hour. Oh, these letters from Steffi postponing engagements — they're getting on my nerves! What fun this evening might have been! Think I'll read Steffi's letter again. There, I've got it. But if I take it out of my pocket, I'll annoy the fellow next to me. — I know what's in it . . . she can't come because she has to have dinner with "him.". . . That was funny a week ago when she was at the garden party with him, and I was sitting opposite Kopetzsky; she was continually flirting with me. He didn't notice a thing — why, it's amazing! He's probably a Jew. Works in a bank. And his black moustache . . . . Probably a lieutenant in the reserve as well! Well, he'd better not come to practice in our regiment! They keep on commissioning too many Jews — that's the cause of all this anti-Semitism. The other day at the club, when the affair came up between the Doctor and the Mannheimers . . . they say the Mannheimers themselves are Jews, baptized, of course . . . they don't look it — especially Mrs. Mannheimer . . . blond, beautiful figure . . . . It was a good party, all in all. Wonderful dinner, excellent cigars . . . . They must have piles of money.

Hooray! It'll soon be over! Yes, the whole chorus is rising . . . looks fine — imposing! — Organ too! I like the organ . . . . Ah! that sounds good! Fine! It's really true, I ought to go to concerts more often . . . . I'll tell Kopetzsky how beautiful it was . . . . Wonder whether I'll meet him at the café today? — Oh Lord, I don't feel like going there; I got enough of it yesterday! A hundred and sixty gulden on one card — it was stupid! And who won all the money? Ballert. Ballert, who needed it least of all . . . . It's Ballert's fault that I had to go to this rotten concert . . . . Otherwise I might have played again today, and perhaps won back something. But I'm glad I've promised myself to stay away from cards for a whole month . . . . Mother'll make a face again when she gets my letter! —Ah, she ought to go and see Uncle. He's rich as Croesus; a couple of hundred gulden never worried him. If I could only get him to send me a regular allowance . . . . But, no, I've got to beg for every crown. Then he always says that crops were poor last year! . . . Wonder whether I ought to spend a two weeks' vacation there again this summer? I'll be bored to death there . . . . If the . . . What was her name? . . . Funny, I can't remember a single name! Oh, yes: Etelka! . . . Couldn't understand a word of German . . . nor was it necessary . . . . There was nothing to say! . . . Yes, it ought to be all right, four-teen days of country air and fourteen nights with

Etelka or someone else . . . . But I ought to be with Papa and Mama for at least a week. She looked badly last Christmas . . . . Well, she'll be over her worries by now. If I were in her place I'd be happy that Papa's been retired on pension. — And Clara'll be married some time. Uncle will contribute something . . . . Twenty-eight isn't so old . . . . I'm sure Steffi's no younger . . . . It's really remarkable: the fast girls stay young much longer. Maretti, who played in *Sans Gêne* recently, — she's easily thirty-seven, and looks . . . Well, I wouldn't have said no! Too bad she didn't ask me . . . .

Getting hot! Not over yet? Ah, I'm looking forward to the fresh air outside. I'll take a little walk around the Ring . . . . Today: early to bed, so as to be fresh for tomorrow afternoon! Funny, how little I think of it; it means nothing to me! The first time it worried me a bit. Not that I was afraid, but I was nervous the night before . . . . Lieutenant Bisanz was a tough opponent. — And still, nothing happened to me! . . . And it's already a year and a half since then! Well, if Bisanz did nothing to me, the doctor certainly won't! Still, these inexperienced fencers are often the most dangerous ones. Doschintzky's told me that on one occasion a fellow who had never

had a sword in his hand before almost killed him;
and today Doschintzky is the fencing instructor of
the militia. — I wonder whether he was as good
then as he is now? . . . Most important of all: keep
cool. I don't feel the least angry now — but he was
impudent — unbelievably impudent. He'd probably not have done it if he hadn't been drinking
champagne . . . . Such insolence! He's probably a
Socialist. All the enemies of law and order are So-
cialists these days. They're a gang . . . . They'd like
to do away with the whole army; but they never
think of who could help them out if the Chinese
ever invaded the country. Fools! I'll have to make
an example of one of them. I was quite right. I'm
really glad that I didn't let him get away with that
remark. I'm furious whenever I think of it! But I
behaved superbly. The Colonel said it was absolutely
correct. I'll get something out of this affair. I know
some who would have let him get away with it.
Muller certainly would have taken it "objectively,"
or whatever they call it. This being "objective" is a
lot of nonsense. "Lieutenant" — just the way in
which he said "Lieutenant" was annoying. "You will
have to admit —" . . . — How did the thing start?
How did I ever start talking to a Socialist? . . . As I

recall it, the brunette I was taking to the buffet was with us, and then this young fellow who paints hunting scenes — what is his name? . . . Good Lord, he's to blame for it all! He was talking about the manœuvers; and it was only then that the Doctor joined us and said something or other I didn't like — about playing at war — something like that — but I couldn't say anything just then . . . . Yes, that's it . . . . And then they were talking about the Military School . . . . Yes, that's the way it was . . . . And I was telling them about a patriotic rally . . . . And then the Doctor said — not immediately, but it grew out of my talk about the rally — "Lieutenant, you'll admit, won't you, that all of your friends haven't gone into military service for the sole purpose of defending our Fatherland!" What a nerve of anyone to dare say a thing like that to an officer! I wish I could remember exactly how I answered him — Oh, yes, something about "fools rushing in where angels fear to tread" . . . Yes, that was it . . . . And there was a fellow there who wanted to smooth over matters — an elderly man with a cold in the head — but I was wild! The Doctor had said it in a tone that meant he was talking about me, and me only. The only thing he could have added was that

they had expelled me from college and for that reason I had to go into military service . . . . Those
people don't understand our point of view. They're
too dull-witted . . . . Not everyone can experience
the thrill I did the first time I wore a uniform . . . .
Last year at the manœuvers — I would have given a
great deal if it had suddenly been in earnest . . . .
Mirovic told me he felt exactly the same way. And
then when His Majesty rode up at the front and the
Colonel addressed us — only a nincompoop
wouldn't have been thrilled by it . . . . And now a
boor comes along who has been a bookworm all
his life and has the temerity to make a fresh
remark . . . . Oh, just wait. Just see how fit you'll
be for the duel! . . .

Well, what's this? It must be over by now . . . .
"Ye, his Angels, praise the Lord" — Surely, that's
the final chorus . . . . Beautiful, really beautiful! And
here I've completely forgotten the girl in the box
who was flirting with me before . . . . Where is she
now? . . . Already gone . . . . That one over there
seems rather nice . . . . Stupid of me — I left my
opera glasses at home. I wish the cute little one
over there would turn around. She sits there so properly. The one next to her is probably her mother . . . .

I wonder whether I ought to consider marriage seriously? Willy was no older than I when he married. He's done well by himself — and always a pretty wife at home . . . . Too bad that just today Steffi had no time! If I only knew where she was. I'd like to have a little tête-a-tête with her. There'd be a fine how-do-you-do! If he'd ever catch me, he'd palm her off on me. When I think what it must cost Fleiss to keep the Winterfeld woman! — and even at that, she's unfaithful to him right and left. Some day she'll get the fright that's coming to her . . . . Bravo, bravo! Ah, it's over . . . . Oh, it feels good to get up and stretch. Well! How long is he going to take to put that opera glass into his pocket?

"Pardon me, won't you let me pass?"

What a crowd! Better let the people go by . . . . Gorgeous person . . . . Wonder whether they're genuine diamonds? . . . That one over there's rather attractive . . . . The way she's flirting with me! . . . Why, yes, my lady, I'd be glad to! . . . Oh, what a nose! — Jewess . . . . Another one. It's amazing, half of them are Jews. One can't even hear an oratorio unmolested these days . . . . Now we're crowding together. Why is that idiot back of me pushing so? I'll teach him better manners . . . . Oh, it's an elderly man! . . . Who's that bowing to me over there? . . . How do you do. Charmed! I haven't the slightest idea who he is . . . . I think I'll go right over to Leidinger's for a bite. Maybe Steffi'll be there after all. Why didn't she write and let me know where she's going with him? She probably didn't know herself. Oh, it's fierce, this day-to-day existence . . . . Poor thing — So, here's the exit . . . . Ah! that one's pretty as a picture! All alone? She's smiling at me. There's an idea — I'll follow her! . . . Now, down the steps . . . . Oh, a Major — a recent graduate — very nice, the way he returned my salute. I'm not the only officer here after all . . . . Where did the pretty girl go? . . . There she is, standing by the banister . . . . Now to the wardrobe . . . . Better not lose her . . . . She's nabbed him already. What a hussy! Having someone call for her, and then laughing at me out of the side of her face! They're all worthless . . . . Good Lord, what a mob there at the wardrobe. Better wait a little while. Why doesn't the idiot take my check?

"Here, Number 224! It's hanging there! What's the matter — are you blind? Hanging there! There! At last . . . . Thank you." That fatty there is taking up most of the wardrobe . . . . "If you please!" . . .

"Patience, patience."

What's the fellow saying?

"Just have a little patience."

I'll have to answer him in kind. "Why don't you allow some room?"

"You'll get there in time." What's he saying? Did he say that to me? That's rather strong! I won't swallow that. "Keep quiet!"

"What did you say?"

That's a fine way to talk! This has got to stop right now.

"Don't push!"

"Shut your mouth!" I shouldn't have said that. That was a bit rough . . . . Well, I've done it now.

"Exactly what did you mean by that?"

Now he's turning around. Why I know him! — Heavens, it's the baker, the one who always comes to the café . . . . What's he doing here? He probably has a daughter or something in the chorus. Well, what's this? — What's he trying to do? It looks as though . . . Yes, Great Scott, he has the hilt of my sword in his hand! What's the matter? Is the man crazy? . . . "You Sir! . . ."

"You, Lieutenant, just be altogether quiet."

What's he saying? For Heaven's sake, I hope no

one's heard it. No, he's talking very softly. . . . Well, why doesn't he let go of my sword? Great God! This is getting rough. I can't budge his hand from the hilt. Let's not have a rumpus here! Isn't the Major behind him? Can anyone notice that he's holding the hilt of my sword? Why, he's talking to me! What's he saying!

"Lieutenant, if you dare to make the slightest fuss, I'll pull your sword out of the sheath, break it in two and send the pieces to your Regimental Commander. Do you understand me, you young fathead?"

What did he say? Am I dreaming? Is he really talking to me? How shall I answer him? But he's in earnest. He's really pulling the sword out. Great God! he's doing it! . . . I can feel it! He's already pulling it! What is he saying? For God's sake, no scandal! — What's he forever saying?

"But I have no desire to ruin your career. . . . So just be a good boy. . . . Don't be scared. Nobody's heard it . . . . Everything's all right . . . . And so that no one will think we've been fighting I'll act most friendly toward you . . . . I am honored, Sir Lieutenant. It has been a pleasure — I am honored."

Good God, did I dream that? . . . Did he really

say that? . . . Where is he? . . . There he goes I
must draw my sword and run him through — Heavens, I hope nobody heard it . . . . No, he talked very
softly — right in my ear. Why don't I go after him
and crack open his skull? . . . No, it can't be done.
It can't be done . . . . I should have done it at
once . . . . Why didn't I do it immediately? . . . I
couldn't . . . . He wouldn't let go of the hilt, and
he's ten times as strong as I am . . . . If I had said
another word he would actually have broken the
sword in two. I ought to be glad that he spoke no
louder. If anyone had heard it, I'd have had to shoot
myself on the spot . . . . Perhaps it was only a dream.
Why is that man by the pillar looking at me like
that? — Did he really hear it? . . . I'll ask him . . . ask
him?! — Am I crazy? — Do I look queer? — I must
be pale as a sheet — Where's the swine? I've got to
kill him! . . . He's gone . . . . The whole place is
empty. . . . Where's my coat? . . . Why I'm already
wearing it . . . . I didn't even notice it . . . . Who
helped me on with it? . . . Oh, that one there. I'll
have to tip him . . . . So. But what's it all about? Did
it really happen? Did anyone really talk to me like
that? Did anyone really call me a fathead? And I
didn't cut him to pieces on the spot? . . . But I

couldn't . . . . He had a fist like iron. I just stood there as though I were nailed to the floor. I think I must have lost my senses. Otherwise, I would have used my other hand . . . . But then he would have drawn out my sword, and broken it, and everything would have been over . . . . Over and done with! And afterwards, when he walked away, it was too late . . . . I couldn't have run my sword through him from the back.

What, am I already on the street? How did I ever get here? — It's so cool . . . . Oh, the wind feels fine! . . . Who's that over there? Why are they looking over at me? I wonder whether they really heard it . . . . No, no one could have heard it . . . . I'm sure of it — I looked around immediately! No one paid any attention to me. No one heard a thing . . . . But he said it anyhow. Even if nobody heard it, he certainly said it. I just stood there and took it as if someone had knocked me silly . . . . But I couldn't say a word — couldn't do a thing. All I did was stand there —, quiet, absolutely quiet! . . . It's awful; it's unbearable; I must kill him on the spot, wherever I happen to meet him! . . . I let a swine like that get away with it! . . . He can tell everybody just exactly what he said to me! . . . No, he wouldn't do that.

Otherwise, he wouldn't have talked so quietly. . . .
He just wanted me to hear it alone! . . . But how do
I know that he won't repeat it today or tomorrow,
to his wife, to his daughter, to his friends in the
café — For God's sake, I'll see him again tomorrow.
As soon as I stop into the café tomorrow, I'll see
him sitting there as he does every day, playing Tarok
with Schlesinger and the fancy flower merchant.
No, that can't happen. I won't allow it to. The moment I see him I'll run him through . . . . No, I can't
do that . . . . I should have done it right then and
there! . . . If I only had! I'll go to the Colonel and
tell him about the whole affair . . . . Yes, right to
the Colonel . . . . The Colonel is always friendly —
and I'll say to him — Colonel, I wish to report, Sir.
He grasped the hilt of my sword and wouldn't let
go of it; it was just as though I were completely
unarmed . . . . What will the Colonel say? — What
will he say? There's just one answer: dishonorable
discharge! . . . Are those recruits over there? Disgusting. At night they look like officers . . . . Yes,
they're saluting! — If they knew — if they really
knew! . . . There's the Hochleitner Café. Probably a
couple of officers in my company are there
now . . . . Perhaps one or more whom I know . . . .

Wonder if it wouldn't be best to tell the first one I meet all about it — but just as if it had happened to someone else? . . . I'm already growing a bit crazy. . . . Where the devil am I walking? What business have I out here in the street? — Where should I go? Wasn't I going to the Leidinger Café? Haha! If I were to sit down with them I'm sure everyone would see what had happened to me . . . . Well, something must happen . . . . But what? . . . Nothing, nothing at all — no one heard it. No one knows a thing. At least for the time being . . . . Perhaps I ought to visit him at his home and beg him to swear to me that he'll never tell a soul. — Ah, better to put a bullet through my head at once. That would be the cleverest way of all — the cleverest! — there's just nothing else left for me — nothing. If I were to ask the Colonel or Kopetzsky, or Blany, or Freidmair: — they'd all tell me the same thing. How would it be if I were to talk it over with Kopetzsky? Yes, that seems the most sensible thing to do. But what about tomorrow — tomorrow — yes, that's right, tomorrow — at four o'clock, in the armory, I'm to fight a duel. But I can't do it, I'm no longer qualified for duelling. Nonsense, nonsense, not a soul knows it, not a soul!

— There are hundreds of people walking around to whom worse things have happened . . . . What about all those stories I've heard about Deckener — how he and Rederow fought with pistols . . . . And the duelling committee decided that the duel could take place at that . . . . But what will the committee decide about me? — Fathead, fathead, and I just stood there and took it —! Great Heavens, it makes no difference whether anyone knows it or not! The chief thing is: I know he said it! I feel as though I'm not the same man I was an hour ago — I know that I'm not qualified for duelling, and that I must shoot myself. I wouldn't have another calm moment in my life. I'd always be afraid that someone might know about it in some way or another, and that some time someone might tell me about this evening's affair! —What a happy man I was an hour ago! . . . Just because Kopetzky gave me a ticket, and just because Steffi postponed her date — destiny hangs on things like that . . . . This afternoon, all was sailing smoothly, and now I am a lost man about to shoot himself . . . . Why am I running this way? No one is chasing me. What's the time there? 1, 2, 3, 4, 5, 6, 7, 8, 9, 10, 11 . . . . Eleven, Eleven . . . . I ought to go and get something to eat . . . . I'll certainly land somewhere. I might go and sit down in some little restaurant where no one would know me. — At any rate, a man must eat even though he kill himself immediately after. Haha! Death is no child's play . . . . Who said that recently? — It makes no difference.

I wonder who'll worry about me most, . . . Mama or Steffi? . . . Steffi, Great God, Steffi! . . . She won't allow anyone to notice how she feels. Otherwise "he" will throw her out . . . . Poor little thing! — At my regiment . . . . No one will have the slightest idea why I did it. They'll all have their theories on why Gustl committed suicide. But no one will hit upon the real solution: that I had to shoot myself because a miserable baker, a low person who just happened to have a strong fist . . . . It's too silly — too silly for words! — For that reason, a fellow like myself, young and fit . . . . Well, they'll all say he didn't have to commit suicide for a silly reason like that. It's a pity! But if I were to ask anyone right now, they'd all give me the same answer . . . . And if I were to ask myself . . . . Oh, the devil, we're absolutely helpless against civilians. People think that we're better off just because we carry swords, and if one of us ever makes use of a weapon, the story goes around that we're all born murderers. The paper will carry a story: "Young Officer Suicide"... How do they always put it?... "Motive Concealed" ... Haha!... "Mourning at his Coffin."... — But it's true. I feel as if I were forever telling myself a story.... It's true.... I must commit suicide. There's nothing else left to do — I can't allow Kopetzsky and Blany to come tomorrow morning and say to me: Sorry, we can't be your seconds. I'd be a fool if I'd give them the chance — fool that I am, standing quietly by and letting myself be called a fathead.... Tomorrow everyone will know it. Fancy myself believing for a moment that a person like that won't repeat it everywhere.... Why, his wife knows it already! Tomorrow everyone in the café will know it. All the waiters will know it. Schlesinger will know it — so will the cashier girl — And even if he promised that he wouldn't tell anybody, he'll certainly tell them the day after tomorrow.... And if not then, in a week from now.... And if he were to get apoplexy tonight, I'd know it.... I'd know it. And I could no longer wear a cape and carry a sword if such a curse were on me!... So, I've got to do it — I've got to do it — what else? — Tomorrow afternoon the doctor might just as well run his sword through me . . . . Things like this have happened before . . . . And Bauer, poor fellow, lost his mind and died three days later . . . . And Brenitsch fell off his horse and broke his neck . . . . And furthermore, there's nothing else to do, not for me anyhow, certainly not for me! — There are men who would take it more lightly . . . . But God, what sort of men are they! . . . Fleischsalcher slapped Ringeiner's face when he caught him with his wife, whereupon Ringeiner quit and is now somewhere out in the country, married . . . . There are women, I suppose, who'll marry people like that! . . . On my word, I'll never shake hands with him if he ever returns to Vienna! . . . Well, you've heard it, Gustl: — life is over for you — finished, once and for all. I know it now, it's a simple story . . . . So! I'll be altogether calm . . . . I've always known it: if the occasion were ever to arise, I'd be calm, altogether calm . . . . But I would never have believed that it would come to this . . . . —That I'd have to kill myself just because a . . . . Perhaps I didn't understand him correctly . . . . He was talking in an altogether different tone at the end . . . . I was simply a little out of my mind on account of the singing and the heat . . . . Perhaps I was momentarily demented, and it's all not true . . . . Not true, haha! Not true! — I can still hear it . . . . It's still ringing in my ears, and I can still feel in my fingers how I tried to move his hand from the hilt of my sword. He's a husky brute . . . . I'm no weakling myself. Franziski is the only man in the regiment who's stronger than I.

Already at the bridge? . . . How far am I running? If I keep on this way I'll be at Kagran by midnight . . . . Haha! . . . Good Lord, how happy we were last September when we entered Kagran. Only two hours more, and Vienna! . . . I was dead tired when we got there . . . . Had slept like a log all afternoon, and by evening we were already at Ronacher's . . . . Kopetzsky and Ladsiner . . . . Who else was along with us at the time? — Yes, that's right . . . that volunteer, the one who told us the Jewish stories while we were marching. Sometimes they're pleasant fellows, these one-year men . . . . But all of them ought to become substitutes. For what sense is there to it: all of us slave for ages, and a fellow like him serves a year and receives the same distinction as we . . . . It's unfair! — But what's it to me? Why bother about it all? A private in the hospital corps counts for more than I do right now.... I no longer belong on the face of the earth.... All is over with me. Honor lost — all lost!... There's nothing else for me to do but load my revolver and... Gustl, Gustl, you're not thinking this out properly! Come to your senses!... There's no way out.... No matter how you torture your brain, there's no way out! — The point is, now that the end is here, behave like an officer and a gentleman so that the Colonel will say: He was a good fellow, we'll always think well of him!... How many companies attend the funeral of a lieutenant?... I really must know that.... Haha! Even if the whole battalion turns out, even if the whole garrison turns out, and they fire twenty salutes, I'll never wake up! Last summer, after the Army Steeple-chase, I was sitting in front of the café with Engel.... Funny, I've never seen the fellow since.... Why did he have his left eye bandaged? I always wanted to ask him, but it didn't seem proper.... There go two artillery-men.... They probably think I'm following that woman.... Does she *have* to solicit me?... Oh, Lord! I wonder how that one can possibly earn a living.... I'd sooner... However, in time of need a person will do almost anything... In Przemsyl

— I was so horrified that I swore I'd never look at a woman again . . . . That was a ghastly time up there in Galicia . . . . Altogether a stroke of fortune that we ever returned to Vienna. Bokonny is still in Sambor, and will stay for ten years more, getting old and grey. . . . What happened to me today would never have happened if I'd remained there myself, and I'd far sooner grow old in Galicia than . . . Than what? Than what? — What is it? What is it? Am I crazy — the way I always forget? — Good God, I forget it every moment . . . . Has it ever happened before that a man within two hours of putting a bullet through his head digresses on all conceivable matters that no longer concern him? I feel as if I were drunk. Haha, drunk indeed! Drunk with death! Drunk with suicide! Ha, trying to be funny! Yes, I'm in a good mood — must have been born with one. Certainly, if I ever told anybody they'd say I was lying. — I feel as if I already had the revolver at my head . . . . Now, I'd pull the trigger — in a second all is over . . . . Not everyone gets over it so easily — others brood over it month after month. My poor cousin, on his back two years, couldn't move, had the most excruciating pains, what a time! . . . Care is the only thing necessary;

to aim well, so that nothing unforeseen happens, as it did to that substitute last year . . . . Poor devil, didn't die, but became blind . . . . What ever happened to him? Wonder where he's living now. Terrible to run around the way he — that is, he can't run around, he's led. A chap like him — can't be more than twenty years old right now. He shot at the girl more accurately . . . . She was dead at once . . . . Unbelievable, the reasons people have for killing. How can anyone be jealous? . . . I've never been jealous in my whole life. At this very moment Steffi is sitting comfortable at the dance hall; then she will go home with "him" . . . . Doesn't mean a thing to me . . . . Not a thing. She has a nicely furnished place — a little bathroom with a red lamp — When she recently came in, in her green kimono . . . . I'll never see the green kimono again — Steffi, herself, I'll never see again — And I'll never go up the fine broad steps in Gusshaus Strasse. Steffi will keep on amusing herself as if nothing had happened; she shan't tell a soul that her beloved Gustl committed suicide. But she'll weep — oh yes, she'll weep. A great many people will weep . . . . Good God, Mama! — No, no I can't think about it. Oh, no, I can't bear to . . . . You're not to think about home at all, Gustl, you understand? Not — at — all.

This isn't bad. I'm now on the way to the Prater. Midnight . . . . That's another thing I didn't think of this morning, that tonight I'd be taking a walk in the Prater . . . . Wonder what the watchman there thinks . . . . Well, I'll walk on. It's rather nice here. No fun to take a bite; no fun in the café. The air is pleasant and it's quiet . . . . Indeed, I'll have a great deal of quiet — as much as I could possibly want. Haha! — But I'm altogether out of breath. I must have been running like crazy . . . . Slower, slower, Gustl, you'll miss nothing, there's nothing more to do, nothing, absolutely nothing! What's this, am I getting a chill? — Probably on account of worrying, and I haven't eaten a thing. What's that beautiful smell? . . . Are the blossoms out yet? — What's today? — The fourth of April. It's been raining a great deal the last few days, but the street is almost entirely bare and it's dark. Hooh! Dark enough to give you the shivers . . . . That was really the only time in my whole life I was scared — when I was a little kid that time in the woods . . . . But I wasn't so little at that . . . . Fourteen or fifteen . . . . How long ago was it? — Nine years . . . . Easily. At eighteen I was a substitute; at twenty a lieutenant and next year I'll be . . . What'll I be next year? What do I mean; next year? What do I mean; next week? What do I mean; tomorrow? . . . What's this? Teeth chattering? Oh! — Well! let them chatter a while. Lieutenant, you are altogether alone right now and have no reason for showing off . . . . It's bitter, oh, it's bitter . . . .

I'll sit on that bench . . . . Ah . . . . How far have I come? — How dark it is! That behind me there, that must be the second cafe . . . . I was in there last summer at the time our band gave a concert . . . . With Kopetzsky and with Rüttner — there were a couple of others along . . . . — Lord, I'm tired . . . . As tired as if I'd been marching for the last ten hours . . . . Yes, it would be fine to go to sleep now. — Ha, a lieutenant without shelter! . . . Yes, I really ought to go home . . . . What'll I do at home? — But what am I doing in the Prater? — Ah, it would be best never to get up at all — to sleep here and never wake up . . . . Yes, that would be comfortable! But, Lieutenant, things aren't going to be as comfortable as that for you . . . . What next? — Well I might really consider the whole affair in orderly sequence . . . . All things must be considered . . . . Life is like that . . . . Well, then, let's consider . . . . Consider what? . . . — No, the air feels fine . . . . I ought to go to the Prater more often at night . . . . That should have occurred to me sooner. It's all a thing of the past — the Prater, the air and taking walks . . . . Well, then, what next? — Off with my cap. It's pressing on my forehead . . . . I can't think properly . . . . Ah . . . . So! . . . Now, Gustl, collect your thoughts, make your final arrangements! Tomorrow morning will be the end . . . . Tomorrow morning at seven . . . seven o'clock is a beautiful hour. Haha! —At eight o'clock when school begins, all will be over . . . . Kopetzsky won't be able to teach — he'll be too broken up . . . . But naturally he'll know nothing about it . . . . He may not have heard of it . . . . They found Max Lippay only in the afternoon, and in the morning he had shot himself, and not a soul heard of it . . . . But why bother about whether Kopetzsky will teach school tomorrow . . . . Ha! — Well, then, at seven o'clock — Yes . . . . Well, what next! . . . Nothing more to consider. I'll shoot myself in my room and then — basta! The funeral will be Monday . . . . I know one man who'll enjoy it: the Doctor. The duel can't take place on account of the suicide of one of

the combatants . . . . Wonder what they'll say at
Mannheimers! — Well, he won't make much of
it . . . . But his wife, his pretty, blond . . . . She was
worth considering . . . . Oh, yes, I would have had
a chance with her if I'd only taken a little better
care of myself . . . . Yes, with her it might have been
something altogether different from Steffi . . . . Be
on your toes all the time: that is, court in the proper
way, send flowers, talk decently . . . not: meet me
tomorrow afternoon at the barracks! . . . Yes, a decent woman like her — that might have been something. The captain's wife at Przemsyl wasn't
decent . . . . I could swear that Lubitzsky and
Wermutek . . . and the shabby substitute — she was
unfaithful with him too . . . . But Mannheimer's
wife . . . . Yes, that would be entirely different. That
would have been an experience that might almost
have made me a different man — she might have
given me more polish — or have given me more
respect for myself — But always that kind . . . and I
began so young — I was only a boy that time on
my first vacation when I was home with my parents in Graz . . . . The Reidl woman was also along
— she was Bohemian . . . . Must have been twice
as old as I — came home only the following

morning . . . . The way Father looked at me . . . .
And Clara. I was most ashamed of all before
Clara . . . . She was engaged at the time . . . . Wonder
why the engagement never materialized. I didn't
worry much about it at the time. Poor thing, never
had much luck — and now she's going to lose her
only brother . . . . Yes, you'll never see me again,
Clara — it's all over. You didn't think, little sister,
did you, when you saw me at the station on New
Year's Day that you'd never see me again? — And
Mother . . . Good God! Mother! . . . No, I can't allow myself to think of it. Ah, if I could only go
home first . . . . Say I have a day's leave . . . . See Papa,
Mama, Clara again before it's all over . . . . Yes, I
could take the first train at seven o'clock to Graz.
I'd be there at one . . . . God bless you, Mama . . . .
Hello, Clara! . . . How goes everything? . . . Well this
is a surprise . . . . But they'll notice something . . . .
Surely, Clara . . . . Clara's a smart girl . . . . She wrote
me such a sweet letter the other day, and I still owe
her an answer — and the good advice she always
gives me. Such a whole-hearted creature . . . . Wonder whether everything wouldn't have turned out
differently if I'd stayed at home. I might have stud-
ied political economy and gone into my uncle's

business . . . . They all wanted me to do that when I was a kid . . . . By this time I'd be happily married to a nice, sweet girl . . . Perhaps Anna — she used to like me a lot . . . . I just noticed it again the last time I was home — in spite of her husband and two children . . . . I could see it, just the way she looked at me . . . . And she still calls me "Gustly," the same way she used to . . . . It will hit her hard when she finds out the way I ended up — but her husband will say: I might have known as much — a no-account like him! — They'll all think it was because I owed money . . . . It's not true. I've paid all my debts . . . except the last hundred and sixty gulden — and they'll be here tomorrow. Well I must see to it that Ballert gets his hundred and sixty gulden — I must make a note of that before I shoot myself . . . . It's terrible, it's terrible! . . . If I only could run away from it all, and go to America where nobody knows about it. In America no one will know what happened here this evening . . . . No one will care. Just recently I read in the paper about Count Runge, who had to leave because of some nasty stories that were going around about him. He now owns a hotel over there and doesn't give a hoot for the whole bunch . . . . And in a couple of

years I might return . . . . Not to Vienna, of
course . . . . Nor to Graz . . . but I could go out to
the farm . . . . And Mama and Papa would a dozen
times rather have it that way — just so long as I stay
alive . . . . And why worry about the other people
at all? Who ever cares about me? — Kopetzsky's the
only one who'd ever miss me . . . . Kopetzsky —
the one who gave me the ticket today . . . and the
ticket's to blame for it all. If he hadn't given it to
me, I wouldn't have gone to the concert, and all
this would never have happened . . . . What happened? It's just as if a whole century had passed —
and it's only two hours ago. Two hours ago someone called me a fathead and wanted to break my
sword. Great God, I'm starting to shout here at midnight! Why did it all happen! Couldn't I have waited
longer until the whole wardrobe had emptied out?
And why did I ever tell him to shut up? How did it
ever slip out of me? I'm generally polite. I've never
been so rude, even to my orderly . . . . But of course
I was nervous: all the things that happened just at
the same time . . . . The tough luck in gambling and
Steffi's eternal stalling — and the duel tomorrow
afternoon — and I've been getting too little sleep
lately, and all the noise in the barracks . . . . I couldn't

keep on standing it forever! . . . Before long I would have become ill — would have had to get a furlough . . . . Now it's no longer necessary. . . . I'll get a long furlough now — without pay — Haha! . . .

How long am I going to keep on sitting here? It must be after midnight . . . . Didn't I hear the clock strike midnight a while ago? — What's that there? A carriage driving by? At this hour? I can already imagine . . . . They're better off than I. Perhaps it's Ballert with his Bertha . . . . Why, of all people, Ballert? — Go ahead, right on! That was a good looking carriage His Highness had in Przemsyl . . . . He used to ride in it all the time on his way to the city to see Rosenberg. He was a good mixer, His Highness — chummy with everyone, a good drinking companion. Those were good times . . . . Although . . . it was in a lonely section and the weather was hot enough in the summer to kill you . . . . One afternoon three men were overcome by the heat . . . . Even the corporal in my own company — a handy fellow he was . . . . During the afternoon we used to lie down naked on the bed. Once Wiesner came into the room suddenly; I must just have been dreaming. I stood up and drew my sword — it was lying next to me . . . . Must have looked funny! . . . Wiesner laughed himself sick. He's now the riding master — sorry I didn't go into the cavalry myself. The old man didn't want me to — it would have been too expensive — but it makes no difference now . . . . Why? — Yes, I know: I must die, that's why it makes no difference — I must die . . . . How then — Look here, Gustl, you especially came down here to the Prater in the middle of the night so that not a soul would bother you — you can think over everything quietly . . . . That's all a lot of nonsense about America and quitting the service, and you haven't brains enough to start on another career. And when you reach the age of a hundred and think back to the time that a fellow wanted to break your sword, and called you a fathead and you stood there and couldn't do a thing — no, there's nothing more to think about — what's happened has happened. — That's all nonsense about Mama and Clara — they'll get over it — people get over everything . . . . Oh, Lord, how Mama wept when her brother died — and after four weeks she never thought of it again. She used to ride out to the cemetery . . . first, every week, then every month, and now only on the days of his death. Tomorrow is the day of my death — April 5th. — Wonder whether they'll take my body to Graz — Haha! The worms in Graz will enjoy it! — But that's not my problem — I'll let others worry about that . . . . Well then, what else is there to worry about? . . . Oh yes, the hundred and sixty gulden for Ballert — that's all decided — then I have no debts to meet. — Are there letters to write? Why? To whom? . . . Say goodbye? The devil I will — it's clear enough that a man's gone after he's shot himself! Everyone will soon notice that he's taken his leave . . . . If people only knew how little the whole thing bothers me, they wouldn't feel sorry — No use pitying me . . . . What have I had out of life? — One thing I'd like to have experienced: being in war — but I would have had to wait a long time for that . . . . Outside of that I've experienced everything. Whether a person's called Steffi or Kunigunde makes no difference . . . . And I've heard all the best operettas — and Lohengrin twelve times — and this evening I even heard an oratorio — and a baker called me a fathead. — Good God, I've had enough! Life's opened up all its secrets to me . . . . Well then, I'll go home slowly, very slowly, there's really no hurry. — I'll rest for a few minutes on the bench here in the Prater, and think about — just nothing at all. I'll never lie down in bed again. I'll have enough time to sleep. — This wonderful air! There'll be no more air . . . .

Well, what's this? — Hey, there, Johann, bring me a glass of fresh water . . . . What's this? . . . Where? . . . Am I dreaming? My head. Oh, Good Lord . . . . I can't see straight! — I'm all dressed! — Where am I sitting? — Holy God, I've been sleeping! How could I have been sleeping? It's already growing light. How long have I been sleeping? I mustn't ask — must look at my watch — can't see a thing . . . . Where are my matches? Won't a single one of them light? . . . Three o'clock, and I'm to have my duel at four. — No, not a duel — a suicide! It has nothing to do with a duel; I must shoot myself because a baker called me a fathead . . . . What, did it actually happen? — My head feels so funny . . . . My throat's all clogged up — I can't move at all — my right foot's asleep. — Get up! Get up! . . . Ah, that's better! It's already growing light, and the air . . . . Just like that morning when I was doing picket duty when we were camping in the woods. I woke up feeling differently that time. There was a different sort of day ahead of me . . . . I wonder whether I get it all straight. There's the street — gray, empty — just now I'm the only person in the Prater. I was here once at four o'clock in the morning with Pansinger. — We were riding. I was on Colonel Mirovic's horse and Pansinger on his own nag. — That was May, a year ago — everything was in bloom — everything was green. Now it's still cold, but Spring will soon be here — it will be here in just a few days. — Lilies-of-the-valley, violets — pity I'll never see them again. Everyone else will enjoy them, but I must die! Oh, it's miserable! And others will sit in the café eating, as if nothing had happened — just the way all of us sat in the café on the evening of the day they buried Lippay . . . . And they all liked Lippay so much . . . . He was more popular in the regiment than I. — Why shouldn't they sit in the café when I kick off? — It's quite warm — much warmer than yesterday and there's a fragrance in the air — the blossoms must be out . . . . Wonder whether Steffi will bring me flowers? — It will never occur to her! She'll just ride out to . . . . Oh, if it were still Adele . . . Adele! I'm sure I haven't thought of her for the last two years . . . . As long as I lived I never saw a woman weep the way she did . . . . That was absolutely the tenderest thing I ever lived through . . . she was so modest, so unassuming. — She loved me, I swear she did. — She was altogether different from Steffi . . . . I wonder why I ever gave her up . . . . It was too tame for me, yes, that was the whole thing . . . . Going out with the same person every evening . . . . then perhaps I was afraid that I'd never be able to get rid of her — she always whimpered so. — Well, Gustl, you could have waited a long time until you found anyone who loved you as much as Adele. Wonder what she's doing now. Well, what would she be doing — probably has someone else now. This, with Steffi, is much more comfortable. I am with her only when I want to be — someone else can have all the unpleasantness — I'll take the pleasant part . . . . Well, in that case I certainly can't expect her to come to the cemetery. Wonder if there's anyone who'd go without feeling obliged to. Kopetzsky, perhaps — and that's all! Oh, it's sad, to have no one . . . . Nonsense! There's Papa and Mama and Clara. It's because I'm a son and a brother . . . . What more is there to hold us together? They like me of course — but what do they know about me? — That I'm in the service, that I play cards, and that I run around with fast women . . . . Anything more? Yes, that I often get good and sick of myself — though I never wrote anything to them about that — perhaps the reason is because I have never realized it myself. Well, Gustl, what sort of stuff are you muttering to yourself? It's just about time to start crying . . . . Disgusting! — Keep in step . . . . So! Whether a man goes to a rendezvous or on duty or to battle . . . . Who was it said that? . . . Oh yes, it was Major Lederer. When they were telling us that time at the canteen about Wingleder — the one who grew so pale before his first duel — and vomited . . . . Yes, a true officer will never betray by look or step whether he goes to a rendezvous or certain death! —Therefore, Gustl — remember the major's words! Ha! — Always growing lighter . . . . What's that whistling there? — Oh yes, there's the North Railroad Station . . . . It's never looked so long before . . . . There are the carriages. Nobody except street cleaners around. They're the last street cleaners I'll ever see — Ha! I always laugh when I think of it . . . . I don't under-stand myself . . . . Wonder whether it's that way with everybody, once they're entirely sure. Four-thirty by the clock at the North Railroad Station . . . . The only question now is whether I'm to shoot myself at seven o'clock railroad time or Vienna time . . . . Seven o'clock . . . . Well, why exactly seven? . . . As if it couldn't be any other time as well . . . . I'm hungry — Lord, I'm hungry — No wonder. . . . Since when haven't I eaten? . . . Since — not since yesterday at six o'clock in the café! When Kopetzsky handed me the check — coffee and two rolls. — Wonder what the baker will say when he hears about it? . . . Damned swine. He'll know — he'll realize what it means to be an Austrian officer — a fellow like that can be beaten in the open street and think nothing of it. And if an officer is insulted even in secret, he's as good as dead . . . . If a rascal like him would only fight a duel — but no, then he'd be very careful — he wouldn't take a chance like that. The fellow keeps on living quietly and peacefully while I — it's the end for me! He's responsible for my death . . . . Do you realize, Gustl, it is he who is responsible for your death! But he won't get off as easily as that! — No, no, no! I'll send Kopetzsky a letter telling him the whole story. . . . Better yet: I'll write to the Colonel. He'll make a report to the officer in command . . . . Just like an official report . . . . Just wait — you think, do you, that a matter like this can remain secret! — You're just wrong. — It will be reported and remembered forever. After that I'd like to see whether you'll venture into the café! — Ha! — "I'd like to see" is good! There are lots of things I'd like to see which unfortunately I won't be able to — Out! It's all over! —

At this moment Johann must be coming to my room. He notices that the Lieutenant hasn't slept at home. — Well he'll imagine all sorts of things. But that the Lieutenant has spent the night in the Prater — that, Good Lord, will never occur to him . . . . Ah, there goes the Forty-fourth! They're marching out to target practice. Let them pass. — So, I'll remain right here . . . . A window is being opened up there. — Pretty creature. — Well I, at least, would want to put something around me, going to an open window. Last Sunday was the last time. I'd never have dreamt that Steffi would be the last. Oh God, that's the only real pleasure. Well, now the Colonel will ride after them in two hours in his grand manner. These big fellows take life easy. — Yes, yes, eyes right! Very good. If you only knew how little I care about you all. Ah, that's not bad at all: there goes Katzer. Since when has he been transferred to the Forty-fourth? — How do you do, good morning!

What sort of a face is he making? Why is he point-ing at his head? — My dear fellow, your skull inter-ests me not at all . . . . Oh, it's that way. No, my good chap, you're mistaken: I've just spent the night in the Prater . . . . You will hear about it in the evening paper. — "Impossible!" he'll say, "Early this morning as we were marching out to target prac-tice I met him on the Prater Strasse" — Who'll be put in command of my platoon? I wonder whether they'll give it to Walter. Well that would be a fine how-do-you-do! A fellow totally devoid of imagi-nation — should have been a plumber. — What, the sun coming up already! — This will be a beau-tiful day — a real Spring day. The devil — on a day like this! — Every cab driver will be in the world at eight o'clock this morning and I — well, what about me? Now really, it would be funny if I lost my nerve at the last minute just because of cab drivers . . . . What's up now? — Why's my heart thumping this way? — Not on account of the cab driver. No, oh no, it's because I haven't eaten since yesterday. But Gustl, be honest with yourself: you're scared — scared because you have never tried it before . . . . But that doesn't help. Being scared never helped anybody. Everyone has to experience it once. Some sooner, some later, and you just happen to have to experience it sooner. As a matter of fact you never were worth an awful lot, so the least you can do is to behave decently at the very end. In fact I demand that you do. I'll have to figure it out — figure out what? . . . I'm always trying to figure out . . . . It's lying in the drawer of my table — loaded — just: pull the trigger — certainly not very complicated!

That girl over there's already going to work . . . the poor girls! . . . Adele also used to have to go to work — I called for her a few times in the evening. When they have a job they don't play around so much with men. If Steffi had only listened to me. I always urged her to become a modiste . . . . Wonder how she'll find out about it? — The newspaper! She'll be angry that I didn't write to her about it. I believe I'm beginning to lose my mind. Why bother about whether she'll be angry or not? How long has the whole affair lasted? . . . Since January . . . . No, it must have begun before Christmas. I brought her some candy from Graz, and she sent me a note at New Year's . . . . Good Lord, that's right, I have her letters at home. Are there any I should have burned? . . . 'Mm, the one about Fallsteiner. If that letter is found — the rascal

will get into trouble. Why should that bother me!
— Well it wouldn't be much of an exertion . . . . But
I can't look through all that scrawl . . . . It would
be best to burn the whole bunch . . . . Who'll ever
need them? They're all junk. — My few books I
could leave to Blany — "Through Night and Ice"
— too bad I'll never be able to finish it . . . . Didn't
have much chance to read these last few
months . . . .

Organ playing? In the church there . . . . Early
Mass — haven't been to one in an age . . . . Last time
it was in February when the whole platoon was
ordered to go. But it didn't mean anything. — I was
watching my men to see if they were religious and
behaving properly . . . . I'd like to go to church . . .
there's something substantial about it after
all . . . . Well, this afternoon I'll know all about it.
Ah, "this afternoon" is good! — what shall I do —
go in? I think it would be a comfort to Mother if
she knew! . . . It wouldn't mean as much to
Clara . . . . Well, in I go. It can't hurt! Organ playing — singing — hm! — what's the matter! I'm
growing dizzy . . . . Oh God, Oh, God, Oh God! I
want somebody whom I can talk to before it happens! — How would it be — if I went to confes-

sion! The Father would certainly open his eyes if he heard me say at the end, "Pardon, Revered Father; I am now going to shoot myself!" ... Most of all I want to lie down there on the stone floor and cry my eyes out .... Oh, no, I don't dare do that. But crying sometimes helps so much .... I'll sit down a moment, but I won't go to sleep again as I did in the Prater! ... — People who have religion are much better off .... Well, now my hands are beginning to tremble! If it keeps on this way, I'll soon become so disgusted at myself that I'll commit suicide out of pure shame! That old woman there — what is she still praying about? ... It would be a good idea to say to her: You, please include me too .... I never learned how to do it properly. Ha! It seems that dying makes one stupid! Stand up! Where have I heard that melody before? — Holy God! Last night! — It's the melody from the oratorio! Out, out of here, I can't stand it any more. 'Pst! Not so much noise letting that sword drag — don't disturb the people in their prayers — so! — It's better in the open .... Light .... The time's always growing shorter. Wish it were over already! — I should have done it at once in the Prater .... I should never go out without a revolver .... If I'd had one yesterday evening.... Good Lord! — I might take breakfast in the café.... I'm hungry. It always used to seem remarkable that people who were doomed to die drank coffee and smoked a cigar in the morning.... Heavens, I haven't even smoked! I haven't even felt like smoking! —This is funny: I really feel like going to the café.... Yes, it's already open and there's none of our crowd there right now... and if there were — it would be a magnificent sign of cool headedness! "At six o'clock he was eating breakfast in the café and at seven he killed himself." — I feel altogether calm again. Walking is so pleasant — and best of all, nobody is compelling me. If I wanted to I could still chuck the whole business.... America.... What do I mean, "whole business"? What is a "whole business"? I wonder whether I'm getting a sunstroke. Oho! — am I so quiet because I still imagine that I don't have to? ... I do have to! I must! No, I will! Can you picture yourself, Gustl, taking off your uniform and beating it, and the damned swine laughing behind your back? And Kopetzky not even shaking hands with you? ... I blush just to think of it. — The watchman is saluting me.... I must acknowledge it.... "Good morning!" There, I've said

"Good morning" to him! . . . It always pleases a poor devil like him . . . . Well, no one ever had to complain about me . . . . Off duty I was always pleasant . . . . When we were at the manœuvers I let off the officers of the Kompagnie Britannika. One time at drill I heard an enlisted man behind me say something about "the damned drudgery" and I didn't even report him. — I merely said to him, "See here, be careful — someone else might hear it, and then you'll be in hot water." . . . The Burghof . . . . Wonder who's on guard today? — The Bosniacs — they look good. Just recently the Lieutenant Colonel said "When we were down there in '78, no one would have believed that they'd ever come up to us the way they have." Good God, that's a place I'd like to have been! Those fellows are all getting up from the bench. I'll salute. It's too bad that our company couldn't have been there — that would have been so much more wonderful — on the field of battle for the Fatherland, than . . . . Yes, Doctor, you're getting off easily! . . . Wonder if someone couldn't take my place? Great God, there's an idea — I'll leave word for Kopetzsky or Wymetal to take my place in the duel! . . . He won't get off as easily as all that! — Oh well, what difference does it make what happens later on? I'll never hear anything about it! — The trees are beginning to bud . . . . I once picked up a girl here at the Volksgarten — she was wearing a red dress — lived in the Strozzigasse — later Roschlitz took her off my hands . . . . I think he still keeps her, but he never says anything about it — probably ashamed of it . . . . Steffi's still sleeping, I suppose . . . . She looks so pretty when she's asleep — just as if she couldn't count to five! — Well, they all look alike when they're asleep! — I ought to drop her a line . . . . Why not? Everyone does it . . . writes letters just before — I also want to write Clara to console Papa and Mama and the sort of stuff that one writes! — And to Kopetzsky. My Lord, I'll bet it would have been much simpler if I'd said goodbye to a few people . . . and the announcement to the officers of the regiment. — And the hundred and sixty gulden for Ballert . . . . Still lots of things to do. Well, nobody insists that I do it at seven . . . . There's still time enough after eight o'clock for being deceased! Deceased! That's the word — Then there's nothing else that a fellow can do.

Ringstrasse — I'll soon be at my café . . . . Funny, I'm actually looking forward to breakfast . . . . Unbelievable. — After breakfast I'll light a cigar, then I'll go home and write . . . . First of all I'll make my announcement to the officers of the regiment; then the letter to Clara — then the one to Kopetzsky — then the one to Steffi. What on earth am I going to write to her? . . . *My dear child, you should probably never have thought . . . .* — Lord, what nonsense! — *My dear child, I thank you ever so much . . . .* — *My dear child, before I take my leave, I will not overlook the opportunity . . . .* — Well, letter writing was never my forté . . . . *My dear child, one last farewell from your Gustl . . . .* — What eyes she'll make! It's lucky I wasn't in love with her. . . . It must be sad if one loves a girl and then . . . . Well, Gustl, let well enough alone: it's sad enough as it is . . . . Others would have come along after Steffi, and finally there would have been one who'd have been worth something — a young girl from a good, substantial family — it might have been rather nice . . . . — I must write Clara a detailed letter explaining why I couldn't do otherwise . . . . *You must forgive me, my dear sister, and please console our dear parents. I know that I caused you all a good deal of worry and considerable pain; but believe me, I always loved all of you, and I* hope that some time you will be happy, my dear Clara, and will not completely forget your unhappy brother . . . . — Oh, I'd better not write to her at all! . . . No it's too sad. I can already feel the tears in my eyes when I think . . . . At least I'll write to Kopetzsky. . . . A man to man farewell, and he'll let the others know . . . . — Already six o'clock — oh no, half past five — quarter to. — If that isn't a charming little face! —The little dear, with her black eyes. I've met her so often in the Florianigasse! — Wonder what she'll say? — And she doesn't even know who I am — she'll only wonder why she doesn't see me any more . . . . Day before yesterday I made up my mind to speak to her the next time I met her. — She's been flirting enough . . . . She was so young — but I'll bet no angel at that! . . . Yes, Gustl! Don't put off til tomorrow what you can do today . . . . That fellow over there probably hasn't slept all night. — Well, now he'll go home comfortably and lie down. — So will I! — Haha! This is getting serious, Gustl! Well if there weren't a little fear connected with it, there'd be nothing to do at all — and on the whole I must say in behalf of myself that I have been behaving very nobly . . . . Where'll I go now? There's my café . . . . They're

— 55

still sweeping . . . . Well, I'll go in.

There's the table where they always play
Tarok . . . . Remarkable, I can't imagine why that
fellow who's always sitting next to the wall should
be the same one who . . . . — Nobody here yet . . . .
Where's the waiter? . . . Ha! —There's one coming
out of the kitchen . . . . Quickly putting on his
apron . . . . It's really no longer necessary! . . . Well,
it is, for him . . . . He'll have to wait on other people
today.

"Good morning, Lieutenant."

"Good morning."

"So early today, Lieutenant?"

"Oh that's all right, — I haven't much time, I'll
just sit here with my cloak on."

"Your order, Sir?"

"A cup of coffee."

"Thank you — right away, Lieutenant."

Ah, there are the newspapers . . . are they out as
early as this? . . . Wonder if there's anything in them
about me? . . . Well what would there be — Think
I'll look and see if there's anything about my com-
mitting suicide! Haha! — Why am I still standing
up? . . . Sit down by the window . . . . He's already
brought in the coffee. There, I'll pull the curtain. I

feel uncomfortable with people gaping in. But no one is passing by. . . . Ah, this coffee tastes good — it wasn't a bad idea, this breakfast! . . . I feel like a new man. — The whole trouble was that I didn't eat anything last night. Why has the fellow come back as soon as this? Oh, he's also brought some rolls . . . .

"Has the Lieutenant already heard?"

"Heard what?" For God's sake, does he know something about it already? . . . Nonsense, it's impossible!

"Herr Habetswallner —" What, what's that? That's the baker's name . . . . What's he going to say now? . . . Has he been here already? Was he here yesterday telling them the whole story? . . . Why doesn't he tell me more? . . . He's going to . . . .

"— had a stroke last night at twelve o'clock."

"What?" . . . I mustn't shout this way . . . . No, I can't allow anybody to notice it . . . . But perhaps I'm dreaming . . . . I must ask him again . . . .

"Who did you say had a stroke?" — Rather good, that! — I said it quite innocently! —

"The baker, Lieutenant. You must know him . . . . Don't you remember the fat fellow who played Tarok with the officers here every afternoon . . . with Herr

Schlesinger? Don't you remember the one who used to sit opposite Herr Wasner — the one in the artificial flower business!"

I'm completely awake — everything seems to check up — and still I just can't believe him. — I'll have to ask him again . . . . Altogether innocently . . . .

"You say that he was overcome by a stroke? . . . How did it happen? Who told you about it?"

"Who could know it sooner than we here, Lieutenant? — That roll you are eating there comes from Herr Habetswallner's own bakery. His delivery man who comes here at half past four in the morning told us about it."

Look out! I mustn't give myself away . . . . I feel like shouting . . . . I'll burst out laughing in a minute. In another second I'll kiss Rudolph . . . . But I must ask him something else! Having a stroke doesn't mean that he's dead . . . . Altogether calmly — why should the baker concern me? — I must glance over the paper while I'm asking the waiter.

"You say he's dead?"

"Why certainly, Lieutenant, he died immediately."

Wonderful, wonderful! . . . It's all because I went to church . . . .

"He went to the theatre last night. On the way out he fell on the stairs — the janitor heard him fall . . . . Well, they carried him to his home, and he died long before the doctor ever arrived."

"That's sad — too bad. He was still in the prime of his life." I said that marvelously — not a soul would notice . . . . And I have to do everything to keep from shouting my lungs out and jumping up on the billiard table . . . .

"Yes, Lieutenant, it is very sad. He was such a lovable gentleman; he's been coming to this place for the last twenty years — he was a good friend of the boss. And his poor wife . . . ."

I don't think I've felt as happy as this as long as I've lived. He's dead — dead! Nobody knows about it, and nothing's happened! — What a piece of luck that I came into the café . . . . Otherwise I'd certainly have shot myself — it's like a benediction from heaven . . . . Where did Rudolph go? Oh, he's talking to the furnace man . . . . — Well, he's dead — dead. I just can't seem to believe it! I'd better go and take a look at him myself. — He was probably overcome by a stroke of anger — couldn't control himself . . . . Well, what difference does it make what he was! The main thing is he's dead, and I can keep on living, and everything's all right! . . . Funny, the way I keep on crumbling the roll — the roll Habetswallner baked himself! It tastes very good too, Herr Habetswallner. Splendid! — Ah, now I'll light a cigar . . . .

"Rudolph! Hey, Rudolph! Don't argue so much with the furnace man."

"What is it, Lieutenant?"

"Bring me a cigar." — I'm so happy, so happy! . . . What am I doing? . . . What am I doing? . . . Something's got to happen, or I'll be overcome by a stroke of joy! In a few minutes I'll wander over to the barracks and let Johann give me a cold rub-down . . . . At half past seven we have drill and at half past nine formation. — And I'll write Steffi to leave this evening open for me! And this afternoon at four . . . . Just wait, my boy, I'm in wonderful trim . . . . I'll knock you to smithereens!

GREEN INTEGER
Pataphysics and Pedantry

Douglas Messerli, *Publisher*

Essays, Manifestos, Statements, Speeches, Maxims,
Epistles, Diaristic Notes, Narratives, Natural Histories,
Poems, Plays, Performances, Ramblings, Revelations
and all such ephemera as may appear necessary
to bring society into a slight tremolo of confusion
and fright at least.

*

MASTERWORKS OF FICTION
Green Integer Books

Masterworks of Fiction is a program of Green Integer
to reprint important works of fiction from all centuries.
We make no claim to any superiority of these fictions
over others in either form or subject, but rather we
contend that these works are highly enjoyable to read
and, more importantly, have challenged the ideas and
language of the times in which they were published,
establishing themselves over the years as among
the outstanding works of their period. By republishing
both well known and lesser recognized titles in this series
we hope to continue our mission bringing our society
into a slight tremolo of confusion and fright at least.

BOOKS IN THIS SERIES

José Donoso *Hell Has No Limits* (1966)
Knut Hamsun *A Wanderer Plays on Muted Strings* (1909)
Raymond Federman *The Twofold Vibration* (1982)
Gertrude Stein *To Do: A Book of Alphabets
and Birthdays* (1957)
Gérard de Nerval *Aurélia* (1855)
Tereza Albues *Pedra Canga* (1987)
Sigurd Hoel *Meeting at the Milestone* (1947)
Leslie Scalapino *Defoe* (1994)
Charles Dickens *A Christmas Carol* (1843)
Michael Disend *Stomping the Goyim* (1969)
Anthony Powell *O, How the Wheel Becomes It!* (1983)
Anthony Powell *Venusberg* (1932)
Arthur Schnitzler *Lieutenant Gustl* (1901)
Toby Olson *Utah* (1987)

GREEN INTEGER BOOKS

3102